The Moonlit Owl

Richard Brown

Illustrated by Stephen Lambert

CAMBRIDGE
UNIVERSITY PRESS

I loved staying in Granny's big old house.

Once, when I was four, I went to stay
with her by myself.

One night, while I was there, Granny read
me a story about badgers.

As I fell asleep, an owl hooted outside.

The next day, I said to Granny,
"Are there any badgers in our woods?"
Granny said, "Yes, I've seen them.
Shall we go and look for them tonight?"

When it got dark, we walked into the
moonlit woods.

Deep in the woods, an owl hooted.
We came to a hole in the roots of a tree.

"This is where the badgers live," whispered
Granny.

We watched and waited for a long time,
but no badgers came out.

I felt sleepy. It was hard to keep my
eyes open.

"We'll go home now," whispered Granny.

On the way home, I said, "I *wish* I'd seen the badgers." I felt sad.

When we got home, I was so tired that
Granny had to help me up the stairs.

Then, I opened the bedroom door and
I saw . . .

. . . an owl. There was an owl on the
window-sill.

For a long time, we watched the moonlit owl.
   Then it saw us.
   "It's going," I said. And the owl flew off
into the moonlight.

I felt happy then.

And, as I fell asleep, the owl hooted far away.